The missing invitation

A first book of halves and quarters

Written by Tim Healey
Illustrated by Margaret Chamberlain

READER'S DIGEST Kids

PLEASANTVILLE, N.Y. · MONTREAL

S quirrel was delighted when a letter arrived for him one morning. It was a party invitation. "Whoopee!" yelled Squirrel. "Look, Rabbit, Bear's having a party and I've been asked to go."

As Squirrel placed the invitation proudly on the mantelpiece, Rabbit began to frown. Why hadn't he been invited too? "I've been friends with Bear as long as Squirrel," he grumbled to himself.

When Squirrel went into the kitchen to make a jug of iced tea, Rabbit snatched the invitation from the mantelpiece. "Dear Squirrel," it read. "Please come to my party. There will be a splendid cake." It was signed: "Bear."

"Pah!" muttered Rabbit, and in a
fit of temper, he tore the invitation
in half. He put the two halves on
the table.

Then Rabbit had another fit of temper and tore up the two halves again, making four quarters.

He still felt cross, so he picked up
the four quarters of the
invitation …

. . . and threw them out of the
window.

A moment later, Rabbit heard a noise at the door, and another letter appeared. This one had Rabbit's name on it, so he opened it. "Dear Rabbit," he read. "Please come to my party. There will be a splendid cake . . ." Signed, "Bear."

Rabbit was invited after all!

"Oh my goodness!" gasped Rabbit. "What have I done?" He had torn up poor Squirrel's invitation and thrown it away. Where had he put the pieces? Just as Rabbit was rushing around the room in a panic, there was a loud knock at the door.

"Helloooo," hooted Owl, marching cheerfully into the room. "Yoooo'll never guess what: I've been invited to Bear's party. There will be a big cake toooo."

"Yes, yes," Rabbit muttered, "we've had invitations as well."

"Well I hope that yoooo'll smarten yourself up first," said Owl. "Your jacket is missing a button. And as for your garden . . . well, it's very untidy.

"I counted four torn-up scraps of paper on the grass," Owl continued. "Quite disgraceful.

Luckily for yoooo, I saw four tidy little mice carry the paper away."

Rabbit rushed to the window and looked out. "What would they want paper for?" he asked, realizing that Owl must have seen the four pieces of the missing invitation.

"Toooo shred up for their nest, I expect," Owl replied, looking at the jug of iced tea.

As Owl sat down to enjoy her iced tea,
Rabbit scampered from the room. "To
shred up for their nest!" he squeaked.
"I tore Squirrel's invitation into four
quarters. And now the mice are going
to shred them up! I must stop them."

Rabbit rushed along a prickly
path . . .

. . . and slid down a slippery bank.

At last he came, puffing and panting, to an old tree. There in the side, among the roots, was the tiny door of the mice's home.

"Knock, knock, knock," he went.

"Who is it?" squeaked four tiny voices.

"It's me . . . Rabbit. I must have
those four pieces of paper back.
Please don't shred them up."

There was silence for a moment. Then a mouse's voice replied, "They are very useful pieces of paper, and we took a lot of trouble to carry them here. If you want them back, you'll have to give us something in return."

"Something in return?" asked Rabbit. "What type of something?"

"Cheese," said another mousy voice. "We'll trade four scraps of paper for four pieces of cheese."

Rabbit dashed back home, up the slippery bank . . .

. . . along the prickly path.

When he got home, Owl and
Squirrel were chatting away
cheerfully, and didn't seem to have
noticed that the invitation was
missing from the mantelpiece.

"Some iced tea, Rabbit?" asked
Squirrel. "You look very hot." But
Rabbit rushed past into the kitchen
without a word.

There he found a big, round block
of cheese. First he cut it in two
halves.

Then he cut it into four quarters.

He put the four quarters into a
brown paper bag and rushed
back to the mice's home.

One by one, the mice trooped out of their hole to exchange their four pieces of the torn invitation for four pieces of cheese.

Back Rabbit ran . . . up the slippery bank . . . along the prickly path.

All the while he tried to
think up a brilliant excuse to
explain why the invitation was
torn into four pieces. Should he
say that the mice had done it?

Could he say that the invitation had blown out of the window into a lawn mower?

As he reached home, Rabbit decided to give the best explanation of all — the truth. "Oh Squirrel," he said as he walked in. "I'm very, very sorry, but I was so disappointed when I thought Bear hadn't invited me to his party that I tore up your invitation."

Rabbit explained about the mice and the cheese, looking hot and flustered from his dashing about. He was covered in mud, and his clothes were torn. Squirrel felt sorry for him, and even Owl was understanding. "Never mind, young felloooow," she hooted. "At least you made up for it by getting the invitation back again."

Owl brushed the mud from
Rabbit's clothes . . .

. . . as Squirrel sewed the rips and tears.

They fitted the four quarters
of the invitation back together.
Then they fixed them with
tape. "Nearly as good as
new," smiled Squirrel.

The next day, Rabbit, Squirrel, and Owl all went together to Bear's party. They sang songs and played games and had a very merry time.

The best part of all was when
Bear carried in his cake.
It certainly was a very splendid
cake indeed. He placed it on the
table in front of his three friends.
First he cut it into two halves ...

. . . then he cut it into four quarters.
"Four quarters for four good
friends," smiled Bear.

A Reader's Digest Kids Book
Published by The Reader's Digest Association, Inc.

Designed and produced by Joshua Morris Publishing, Inc.

Printed in Hong Kong

94 95 96 97 10 9 8 7 6 5 4 3 2 1